Discard

X Marks the Spot!

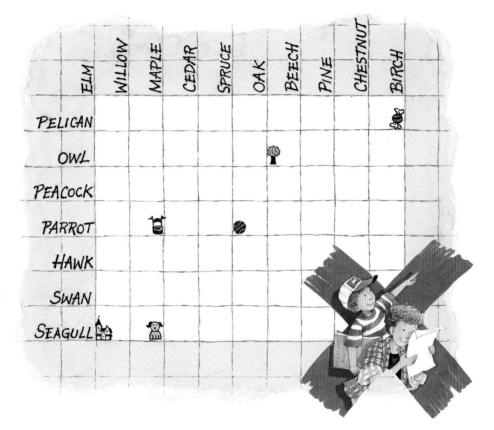

by Lucille Recht Penner
Illustrated by Jerry Smath

The Kane Press
New York

To Lily Dorothy Lorenzen,
—L.R.P.

To Cliff (Bubo) Williams,
—J.S.

Book Design/Art Direction: Roberta Pressel

Library of Congress Cataloging-in-Publication Data

Penner, Lucille Recht.
    X marks the spot / Lucille Recht Penner ; illustrated by Jerry Smath.
      p.   cm. — (Math matters.)
    Summary: Upon moving to their grandfather's house, two boys discover a treasure
    map in the attic and must learn how to use it in order to find their surprise.
    ISBN 1-57565-111-4 (pbk. : alk. paper)
    [1. Buried treasure—Fiction. 2. Moving, Household—Fiction. 3. Maps—Fiction. 4.
      Graphic methods—Fiction.] I. Smath, Jerry, ill. II. Title. III. Series.
    PZ7.P38465 Xm 2002
    [E]—dc21
2001038801   CIP
                                                                               AC

10 9 8 7 6 5 4 3 2 1

First published in the United States of America in 2002 by The Kane Press.
Printed in Hong Kong.

Why do people have to move? We just did and I don't like it one bit. Neither does my little brother, Leo. But Mom thinks it's great.

"Why did we have to move to a boring old house in a boring old town?" I complain.

"Now, Jake," Mom says, "this house belonged to Grandpa. He lived here his whole life until he moved to Florida. Isn't that exciting?"

"I guess so," I say—but I'm just being nice.

Leo and I go outside. A bunch of seagulls dive right over our heads. "Wow!" Leo says. He gets excited about every little thing.

The mail comes. We get a postcard from Grandpa. I read it out loud.

Hi, Jake and Leo! I hope you like the house. It's full of surprises. Check out the attic. Love, Grandpa

We run up to the attic and look around. It's full of old junk. A stuffed owl. Some wooden trunks. A statue of some guy. I'm getting bored.

Then I see a shiny orange folder on the
window sill. It says TREASURE MAPS.

"Treasure!" I say. I grab the folder. A letter
falls out.

"Listen, Jake," says Leo. "READ BEFORE YOU SEARCH!"

I open the folder. There are three maps and some directions:

- Start at zero.
- First go across.
- Then go up.
- Watch for clues.

"A treasure hunt!" shouts Leo.

"Let's get started!" I tell him.

We look at the first map.

"How do we read this?" Leo asks. He turns the map upside down. He turns it around.

"See the left-hand corner at the bottom?" I say. "That's a picture of this house. We start here. I bet that big X marks the treasure."

We go outside. I stare at the first map again.

"What do we do now, Jake?" asks Leo.

"I'll tell you in a minute," I say. "Hold your horses."

Actually, this map is not so easy to figure out after all.

Suddenly I get it. "All the lines on the map are streets," I tell Leo. "Our house is at the corner of Elm Street and Seagull Street."

"I see," Leo says. "Our house is at zero."

We count two lines across, then three lines up, to the X.

"That's five blocks," I say. "Not far to walk."

Mom comes to the door. I ask her if we
can go explore, but I don't tell her about
the treasure. I want her to be surprised.

"This looks like a nice town," I say.
Mom gives me a funny look.

"I'm glad you're starting to like it," she
says. "Be home by supper time."

Leo and I walk along Seagull Street.
We count each street we come to. One:
Willow Street. Two: Maple Street.

"That dog likes me," Leo says.

"We'll come back later," I say. "Now
we have to walk up Maple Street."

We turn the corner onto Maple. First we cross Swan Street, then Hawk Street.

"There's a wishing well on Parrot Street," I say. "That must be X!"

"This is nice, but it isn't a treasure,"
says Leo.

"No, it isn't," I say, "but we can wish we
find the treasure."

We close our eyes. I wish hard.

"What if there is no treasure?" Leo asks.
"Grandpa's always joking around."

"Not about this," I tell him.

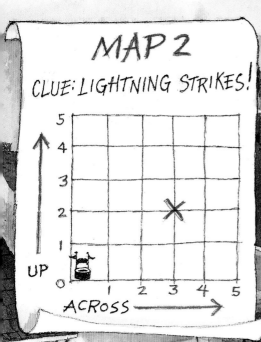

MAP 2

CLUE: LIGHTNING STRIKES!

UP

ACROSS

We look at Map 2. This time the wishing well is at zero. So we start there. We walk three blocks along Parrot Street.

Some boys are shooting baskets. They wave to us. I might like it here after all.

We turn up Oak Street—two blocks to go. Leo is walking slowly. "It might be diamonds," I tell him. He walks faster.

After we cross Peacock Street, we come to Owl Street. We both look up. And up. There's an oak tree on the corner. It's the biggest tree I ever saw. The branches on the top are black.

YE OLDE
OAK TREE
PLANTED IN 1889
STRUCK BY LIGHTNING
1937 and 1991

"That tree is creepy," Leo whispers. "Let's go home."

"Are you kidding?" I yell. "We can't go home without the treasure."

"I bet there is no treasure," Leo says. But he looks at the third map with me.

This time the oak tree is at zero. I put my hand over the map. "Don't look," I say to Leo. "I'll give you a clue. Four, one."

"Four, one," Leo says. "That's easy. We go four streets across and one street up."

"Yes!" I say.

MAP 3
CLUE: SWEETS TO THE SWEET!

UP

ACROSS →

We walk along Owl Street for four blocks. Then we walk up one. There's a candy store on the corner.

"Sweets!" I yell. "This is X!"

We go into the store. A sign inside says
THE GREATEST CANDY STORE EVER!
I believe it. I never saw so much candy in
one place. I'd like to buy one of everything,
but I just have fifty cents.

"What do you want, Leo?" I ask.

"One of those," he says.

"Two giant gummy bears, please," I say to the man behind the counter.

"Thanks, Jake!" says Leo.

"Jake and Leo," the man says. "Could you be Jake and Leo Byrd?"

"Yes," we tell him.

The man reaches under the counter and brings out a key.

"Someone left this for you," he says.

The key is big. It shines like gold. What
is it for? I look at the envelope. It says:

No peeking!

Don't open until you get home.
Hold onto the key. You'll need it!

We hurry down Birch Street and turn right on Seagull Street. We're starting to know our way around this town.

The minute we're home I tear open the envelope. Inside it says: *Look in the backyard behind the rock under the tree.*

We find a little door right in the ground!
I pull it open. There are steps going down.

"Come on," I say to Leo. "I'll go first."

I am so excited I almost fall down the
steps. There is another door at the bottom.
I fit the key in the lock. "This is it," I say.
I take a deep breath and open the door.

We're in a little stone room. A hidden room.
I flip on a light switch.
   "Wow!" says Leo.